HENRY

JAMES

PERCY

MEET ALL THESE FRIENDS IN BUZZ BOOKS:

Thomas the Tank Engine
The Animals of Farthing Wood
Biker Mice from Mars
Winnie-the-Pooh
Fireman Sam
Rupert
Babar

First published 1992 by Buzz Books
an imprint of Reed Children's Books
Michelin House, 81 Fulham Road, London SW3 6RB
and Auckland, Melbourne, Singapore and Toronto
Reprinted 1993, 1994, 1995

ISBN 1 85591 208 2

Printed and bound in Italy by Olivotto

PERCY'S PREDICAMENT

buzz books

While Thomas is away being mended, the other engines are very busy. . . .

Daisy the diesel railcar enjoyed her work in the countryside but she was still very lazy and stubborn.

One day, Toby brought Henrietta to the station where Percy was shunting.

"Hello, Percy," said Toby. "I see Daisy's left the milk again."

"I'll have to make a special journey with it, I suppose. Anyone would think I'd nothing to do," grumbled Percy.

"Tell you what," replied Toby, "I'll take the milk and you can fetch my trucks."

Their drivers and the station master
agreed, and both engines set off. Percy went
to the quarry and began ordering the trucks
about.

The trucks grumbled to each other. "This is Toby's place. Percy's got no right to poke his funnel up here and push us around."

They whispered and passed the word. "Pay Percy out! Pay Percy out!"

At last they were all arranged. "Come along," puffed Percy. "No nonsense."

"We'll give him nonsense!" giggled the trucks, but they followed so quietly that Percy thought they were under control.

Suddenly he saw a notice ahead: ALL
TRAINS STOP TO PIN DOWN BRAKES.

"Peep! Peep!" whistled Percy. "Brakes,
Guard, please!" But before he could check
them the trucks surged forward.

"On! On!" they cried.
"Help! Help!" whistled Percy.

The man on duty at the crossing rushed
to warn the traffic with his red flag. But he
was too late to switch Percy to the
'runaway' siding.

Frantically trying to grip the rails, Percy slid into the yard. The brakevan and some trucks stood in his way. "Peeep! Peeep! Look out!" he whistled.

His driver and fireman jumped clear. Percy whistled and there was a splintering crash! The brakevan was in smithereens. Percy, still whistling fit to burst, was perched on some trucks.

Next day the Fat Controller arrived. Toby and Daisy had helped to clear the wreckage, but Percy remained on his perch of trucks.

"We must now try," said the Fat Controller, "to run the branch line with Toby and a diesel. Percy, you have put us in an *awkward predicament.*"

"I am sorry, sir," replied Percy.

"You can stay there till we are ready," said the Fat Controller. "Perhaps it will teach you to be careful with trucks."

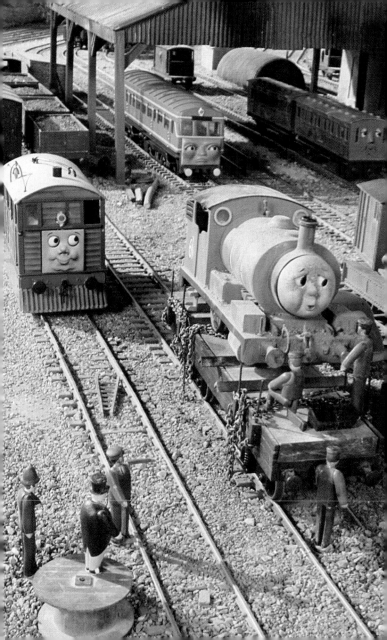

Percy sighed. The trucks groaned beneath his wheels. He quite understood about awkward predicaments.

The Fat Controller spoke severely to
Daisy, too. "My engines must work hard. I
send lazy engines away." Daisy was
ashamed.

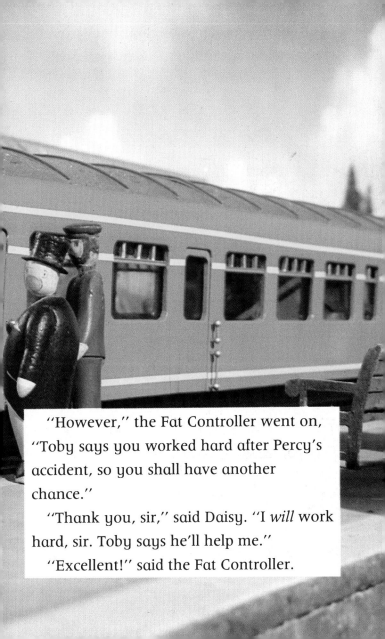

"However," the Fat Controller went on, "Toby says you worked hard after Percy's accident, so you shall have another chance."

"Thank you, sir," said Daisy. "I *will* work hard, sir. Toby says he'll help me."

"Excellent!" said the Fat Controller.

The next day Thomas came back from being mended, and Percy was sent away.

Annie and Clarabel were delighted to see Thomas again, and he took them for a run at once.

Thomas, Toby and Daisy are now all friends, and Toby has taught Daisy a great deal. She often takes the milk for Thomas; and when Toby is busy, she takes Henrietta.

That shows you, doesn't it!

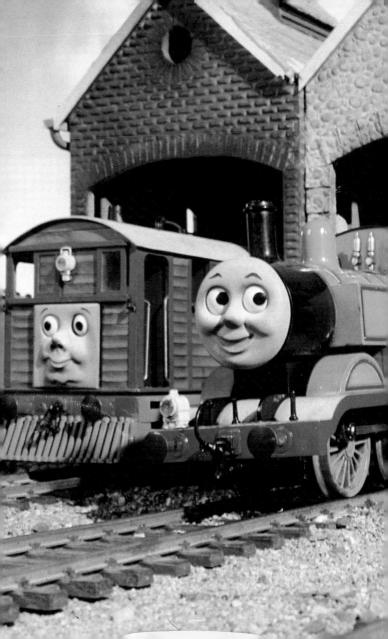

THOMAS

EDWARD

GORDON